YASMIN

The Football Star

written by
SAADIA FARUQI

illustrated by
HATEM ALY

raintree

a Capstone company — publishers for children

To Mariam for inspiring me, and Mubashir
for helping me find the right words—S.F.

To my sister, Eman, and her amazing girls,
Jana and Kenzi—H.A.

Raintree is an imprint of Capstone Global Library Limited, a company
incorporated in England and Wales having its registered office at
264 Banbury Road, Oxford, OX2 7DY – Registered company number:
6695582

www.raintree.co.uk
myorders@raintree.co.uk

Text © Capstone Global Library Limited 2021
The moral rights of the proprietor have been asserted.

Edited by Kristen Mohn
Designed by Lori Bye and Kay Fraser
Original illustrations © Capstone Global Library Limited 2021
Picture research by Jo Miller
Production by Tori Abraham
Originated by Capstone Global Library Ltd

978 1 4747 9367 4

British Library Cataloguing in Publication Data
A full catalogue record for this book is available from the British
Library.

Acknowledgements
Design Elements: Shutterstock: Art and Fashion, rangsan paidaen

Printed and bound in India

TABLE OF CONTENTS

CHAPTER 1

A new coach

It was time for PE, and the headmaster, Mr Nguyen, had some news.

"Children, we have a new PE teacher," he said. "Please welcome Miss Guidu to our school!"

"Welcome, Miss Garcia!" the children all said together.

Yasmin looked at the new coach. She looked very important with her whistle.

"What are we playing today?" Ali asked, jumping up and down. "Four square? Freeze tag?"

Miss Garcia shook her head. "Football!" she announced. She lifted a football over her head.

Ali cheered. "Hooray! I love football!"

Yasmin frowned. She'd watched lots of football on TV with Baba. The players kicked and elbowed and fell down a lot. It looked dangerous.

"I've never played football before," she said quietly.

Miss Garcia heard her. "I'm here to teach you," she replied. "It's good to try new things."

Yasmin groaned.

CHAPTER 2

Excuses

Miss Garcia explained the rules of the game. Then she showed the children some moves.

She stopped the ball with her feet. "This is called trapping," she said.

She kicked the ball while running. "And this is dribbling!"

"Now it's your turn," Miss Garcia said.

Ali already knew how to play. He kicked the ball as hard as he could into the goal.

Yasmin wondered if it hurt his feet to kick like that.

Emma bounced the ball off her knee. That looked like it *really* hurt.

Yasmin stayed near Miss Garcia. "Can I be a supporter?" she asked. "I can cheer really loudly."

Miss Garcia shook her head. "Everyone has to play."

Yasmin watched the others kick and dribble and trap. One boy tripped and fell.

"Can I be the water girl?" she asked. "Everyone looks thirsty."

"No, Yasmin."

Miss Garcia blew her whistle loudly and clapped. "Ready for a game?"

She put the children into teams.

"Can I be the referee? I remember all the rules you taught us," Yasmin begged.

Miss Garcia pointed to the net. "You get to be the goalkeeper," she said firmly.

"*Goalkeeper*?" Yasmin asked with a gulp.

She remembered how Ali
had kicked the ball into the net.
Goalkeeper looked like the most
dangerous job of all.

CHAPTER 3

The goalkeeper

Yasmin stood inside the goal.

She wanted to hide.

Ali kicked the ball. Yasmin

ducked. The ball went straight into

the net. Ali's team cheered.

"Goalkeepers can use their

hands," Miss Garcia reminded.

Soon Ali's team kicked the ball towards the goal again. This time Yasmin jumped to catch it. She missed.

"Goal!" shouted Ali.

Miss Garcia called out, "Good try, Yasmin!"

Yasmin got ready again.

Soon Ali's ball came right at her feet. She rushed towards it – and tripped. But she stopped the ball!

"You did it, Yasmin!" Emma cheered. "You saved the ball!"

Yasmin got up slowly. "I did?"

Miss Garcia gave her a high five. "Well done, Yasmin!"

"You're the star of the team, Yasmin!" Emma said. "Can you teach me that move you did?"

"You were just like the professionals on TV!" Ali said.

Yasmin grinned and wiped
the sweat off her face.

"It wasn't even that
dangerous," she told them.

Miss Garcia offered her a bottle of water. "*I'll* be the water girl," she said.

Yasmin gulped down the water.

"Thanks, Coach," she said. "Who's ready to play again?"

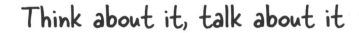

Think about it, talk about it

* Yasmin is worried about trying something that is new and scary to her. Think of a time you tried something new. How did you give yourself courage?

* If you were on Yasmin's football team, what name would you give your team? Why?

* Yasmin watches football with her father. Is there a sport or activity that your parents have shared with you? What activity would you like to do with your parents if you could pick anything?

Learn Urdu with Yasmin!

Yasmin's family speaks both English and Urdu. Urdu is a language from Pakistan. You may already know some Urdu words!

baba father

hijab scarf covering the hair

jaan life; a sweet nickname for a loved one

kameez long tunic or shirt

lassi yogurt drink

mama mother

nana grandfather on mother's side

nani grandmother on mother's side

salaam hello

shukriya thank you

Pakistani fun facts

Yasmin and her family are proud of their Pakistani culture. Yasmin loves to share facts about Pakistan!

Location

Pakistan is on the continent of Asia, with India on one side and Afghanistan on the other.

Population

Pakistan's population is more than 200,000,000 people. It is the world's sixth-most-populous country.

Sport

The most popular sport in Pakistan is cricket. Football is also very popular there.

Pakistan is the world's largest producer of handsewn footballs. The city of Sialkot makes about 40 per cent of the world's footballs each year.

Design your own football top!

SUPPLIES:

- tracing paper or other lightweight paper
- pencil
- felt tips or coloured pencils
- scissors
- tape

STEPS:

1. Lay the paper over this page and trace the front of the top.

2. Use felt tips or coloured pencils to create a design on the top. What colours and designs will your team have? What will your team name be?

3. Cut out your top and tape it to your mirror or a notebook to show your team spirit!

About the author

Saadia Faruqi is a Pakistani American
writer, interfaith activist and cultural
sensitivity trainer previously profiled
in *O Magazine*. She is editor-in-chief
of *Blue Minaret*, a magazine for
Muslim art, poetry and prose. Saadia
is also author of the adult short story
collection, *Brick Walls: Tales of Hope
& Courage from Pakistan*. Her essays
have been published in *Huffington Post*,
Upworthy and *NBC Asian America*. She
lives in Texas, USA, with her husband
and children.

Hatem Aly is an Egyptian-born illustrator whose work has been featured in multiple publications worldwide. He currently lives in beautiful New Brunswick, Canada, with his wife, son and more pets than people. When he is not dipping cookies in a cup of tea or staring at blank pieces of paper, he is usually drawing books. One of the books he illustrated is *The Inquisitor's Tale* by Adam Gidwitz, which won a Newbery Honor and other awards, despite Hatem's drawings of a farting dragon, a two-headed cat and stinky cheese.

Join Yasmin on all her adventures!

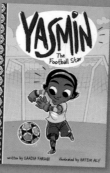

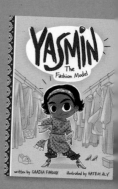

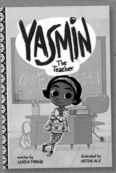

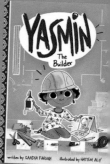